TREETOPS CLASSICS

White Fang

WRITTEN BY JACK LONDON

Adapted by Caroline Castle and Alison Sage
Illustrated by Geoff Taylor

OXFORD
UNIVERSITY PRESS

OXFORD
UNIVERSITY PRESS

is a department of the University of Oxford.
It furthers the University's objective of excellence in research, scholarship,
and education by publishing worldwide in

Oxford   New York

Auckland   Cape Town   Dar es Salaam   Hong Kong   Karachi
Kuala Lumpur   Madrid   Melbourne   Mexico City   Nairobi
New Delhi   Shanghai   Taipei   Toronto

With offices in

Argentina   Austria   Brazil   Chile   Czech Republic   France   Greece
Guatemala   Hungary   Italy   Japan   Poland   Portugal   Singapore
South Korea   Switzerland   Thailand   Turkey   Ukraine   Vietnam

Oxford is a registered trade mark of Oxford University Press
in the UK and in certain other countries

British Library Cataloguing in Publication Data

Data available

ISBN: 978-0-19-911762-8

13 15 17 19 20 18 16 14

Cover illustration by Geoff Taylor

Inside illustrations by Geoff Taylor

**Printed in Malaysia by
MunSang Printers Sdn Bhd**

Paper used in the production of this book is a natural, recyclable product
made from wood grown in sustainable forests. The manufacturing process
conforms to the environmental regulations of the country of origin.

Contents

CHAPTER I

The she-wolf

As night fell, Henry and Bill heard the first cry. A horrible wail, terrifying in the stillness. The two men looked at each other. Then another cry came, and another. Wolves!

'They're after us, Henry,' said Bill.

'Best set up camp and get the fire started,' said Henry. 'They don't like fire.'

The two men ate their food while the dogs huddled together.

'Not like them dogs to stay so close to camp,' said Bill.

At that moment, more shrill wolfish cries ripped the air.

'They got ears, our dogs,' said Henry. 'They know where they're safest. They'd rather eat dinner, than *be* dinner!'

Bill looked thoughtful. 'Henry,' he said, 'how many dogs we got?'

'Six. You know we got six!'

'Yeah, we got six dogs. I gave one fish to each dog but I'm telling you, Henry, I was *one fish short!*'

Bill stopped and looked at his friend, waiting for the full meaning of what he had said to sink in.

'You must have counted wrong,' said Henry.

'I got out six fish, and had to go back for another for old One-ear,' said Bill. 'That's *seven* fish. *Seven* dogs had fish. I'm telling you the truth.'

Henry counted the dogs again. 'Well, there's six now,' he said, looking at his friend as if he was mad.

Bill shook his head. 'I saw seven, Henry. I saw *seven* dogs.'

Henry sighed. 'Bill, I reckon this place is getting to you. You're losing your grip. Now let's get some sleep.'

Close by, a pair of eyes, like burning coals, broke the darkness. Then another pair, and another.

Next morning, the two men woke early. Bill counted the dogs.

'Henry,' he said. 'How many dogs we got?'

'Ten,' joked Henry. 'I guess you're seeing *ten* dogs now, Bill!'

'Wrong!' cried Bill. 'We got *five*. Old Fatty's gone.'

'Gone!' cried Henry, rushing out to count the dogs. Bill was right. There *were* only five dogs.

'That old fool dog, Fatty,' sighed Bill. 'He must have run out into the night and straight into their jaws.'

'Even a fool dog shouldn't commit suicide like that,' said Henry. 'Still, he never was the sharpest card in the pack, that Fatty.'

The next evening, Henry was heating up supper when he heard a sharp squeal of pain. Bill was standing over the dogs with a stick in his hand.

'I got a whack at it,' he said.

'What did it look like?' asked Henry.

'It looked like a wolf,' said Bill. 'But it acted more like a dog.'

'Must be a tame wolf,' said Henry. '*Must* be, to come right into camp at feeding time.'

That night, the circle of burning eyes appeared in the blackness once more. Only this time they drew closer.

'I wish we was back home, right now!'

muttered Henry. 'I wish we'd never set foot out here.'

In the morning, another dog was gone. Froggy. The strongest dog in the pack. 'And he was no fool,' Bill said.

That night, a long shadow glided right into the camp. Then all of a sudden, it moved into the firelight. It was a she-wolf.*

'That's the one I walloped,' whispered Henry. 'She's been leading our dogs away.'

There was a loud crack as a log fell into the fire, and the she-wolf vanished. The following morning, another dog, Spanker, was gone.

Back on the trail, Henry stopped suddenly and gasped. In plain view, stood the she-wolf from the night before.

'It's her!' gasped Bill. This was the creature that had tricked half of their dogs into the jaws of the rest of the wolf pack. And now it was hunting them.

It was large for a wolf, and an odd reddish-grey colour. It glared at them hungrily.

'Must be some kind of wolf-dog,' said Henry.

Bill had had enough. 'I can't stand it,' he screamed. 'She's not getting any more of our dogs!' The creature turned and ran into the forest, and before Henry could stop him, Bill stumbled after it.

That was the last Henry saw of his friend. Later that day, a search party found Henry and the last of his dogs, crouching in his blankets, half mad with cold and fear.

CHAPTER 2

———◆———

The little grey cub

She-wolf had indeed led the pack on their
desperate hunt for food. Now she led them
away from the search party. She knew this
meant danger. Running with her was her
new mate, an old battle-scarred wolf with
one eye.

One day, they split from the pack to
hunt together. But She-wolf was restless.
She seemed to be looking for something,
stopping now and again to search rocks and
overhanging banks.

Arriving at the mouth of a cave, she sniffed,
looked around, and then crept through its

narrow entrance. It was small, but cosy and dry. She-wolf lay down. This was the place she'd been looking for.

Old One-eye went in search of food, but he was unlucky and came back with nothing. At the mouth of the cave, something made him stop dead. Faint, strange sounds were coming from inside. Then came a warning snarl from his mate.

He slowly crept inside. Snuggled between She-wolf's legs were five tiny, whimpering bundles.

She-wolf eyed him, growling. These were her first cubs but instinct* told her that some fathers would kill their helpless newborns.

But she had nothing to fear from One-eye. He was flooded with a fatherly instinct to feed his cubs, and he set off again to hunt.

When he returned with food, She-wolf let him come a little closer to the cubs. He was doing what a wolf father should. He was helping to look after the babies they had brought into the world.

One of the cubs was different from his brothers and sisters who had their mother's reddish fur. He alone had the pure grey wolf coat of his father. His rasping growl was the loudest and he could roll the other cubs over with a quick swipe of his paw.

The first month of his life he spent snuggling into the warmth of his mother. Never moving far from her side, his whole world was the shadowy safety of the cave.

Then one day, he noticed that one wall of the cave was different. This was the cave entrance that let in a little light. As time passed, he longed to go towards that wall of light. But when he tried, his mother gave him a sharp whack on his nose. She knew he was too young to go outside.

This was his first lesson – that taking risks can be painful!

Then came a time when there was no food for the little family and One-eye and She-wolf grew weak with hunger. The cubs simply curled up and went to sleep. Four of them, the little grey cub's brothers and sisters, would never wake again. Then, there was no more play-fighting. He had to play alone.

Then one day, his father stopped coming through the wall of light. Only She-wolf knew the reason. Following One-eye's usual trail – the left fork by the stream – she had found his body under a tree. It was clear there had been a huge fight and that the most vicious of creatures, the lynx,* was to blame.

She felt the loss deeply, but knew that life must go on. She had her cub to feed and protect.

Motherhood is the most powerful force in nature. There would come a time when She-wolf would again take the left fork to the lynx's lair* – for the sake of her little grey cub.

CHAPTER 3

In the big wide world

The day came that the little cub finally went through the wall of light which was the entrance to the cave. He was growing up and he simply *had* to know what lay beyond.

At first, he was almost blinded by the brightness of the big, wide world. But when nothing happened, he forgot to be scared.

He sniffed at the grass. Then he scrambled onto a fallen tree trunk, but the rotten bark gave way and he went tumbling. He fell right into a nest of chicks. At first he was terrified, but he was a born hunter and without even thinking, he began catching and eating them. It was a wonderful game, and how clever he was!

Then all of a sudden, the mother hen returned in a feathered frenzy.

It was his first battle! He was a fierce little wolf and he was afraid of nothing. He growled at her.

She gave him a violent peck on his nose. Sensing he didn't know how to defend himself, the mother bird pecked again and again at his poor nose. He began to whimper. He didn't like this at all! The fight went out of him and he scampered off shamefully to hide in the bushes.

As he lay down, he felt a rush of air and a huge, winged creature swept past. A hawk! It had barely missed him. Then he saw the hawk snatch up the mother hen in its powerful claws. He lay there for a long time, shivering.

That was another big lesson. Live things were food, but some of them could hurt. It was better to eat little things. He felt a rush of pride – he had caught his own food, and he had fought a big bird and would do it again.

Then he remembered his mother. Suddenly, he wanted her more than anything. He felt lonely and small and desperate to be home.

Back in the cave, he anxiously awaited his mother. She was out looking for him. When she returned she was too overjoyed to find him safe to punish him.

She licked him and then curled around him, and they both drifted off to sleep.

CHAPTER 4

——◆——

Tooth and claw

The cub learned quickly. He held grudges too!
If he met a mother hen he would fly into a
fury, remembering the pecks on his nose from
his first day out of the cave.

Famine* came again and for a while, neither
mother nor cub had anything to eat. Then
one day, She-wolf brought home some meat!
It was strange stuff, different from anything
the cub had smelled or tasted before. And it
was all for him! Little could he know that his
mother had taken the left fork by the stream,
by the lair of the lynx, and stolen a kitten.
As he finished his meal, he heard his mother

snarling in a strange and terrible way. He shivered with fear.

The lynx was mad with rage at the loss of her child and she had tracked She-wolf to her cave.

In the glare of the afternoon light, the lynx crouched at the cave entrance. A rasping scream left no doubt what she meant to do. The cub and his mother were trapped!

The lynx hurled herself inside the cave, and She-wolf leaped upon her.

Snarling and screeching, the two mothers fought like demons,* the lynx ripping and tearing with her teeth and claws, She-wolf using her teeth alone.

Seeing his mother in such danger, the cub sank his teeth into the wild cat's leg. Then he clung on for dear life. Although he didn't know it, this is probably what saved their lives. The lynx lashed out at the cub, ripping his shoulder, but he had slowed her down. After a brief, vicious scrap, She-wolf put an end to her once and for all.

They had won, but at a price.

The cub licked his mother's wounds. He knew she was weak and sick. For a week she never left the cave.

Then at last, her strength returned and she was ready to hunt again. This time, the cub went with her. She-wolf noticed a change in her child. He was full of confidence from their victory over the lynx. They had fought a wild cat and lived!

The cub now knew another law of the wild – eat or be eaten: kill or be killed.

CHAPTER 5

A new life

The cub came upon them suddenly. Taking a different path down to the stream, he smelled a strange scent. In front of him were five, live creatures. It was his first sight of men.

But the live things did not show their teeth and growl. They just sat there, silent and mysterious. The cub's instincts told him to turn and run, but a new feeling made him stay. He was spellbound by a sense of mastery and power.

A man got up and walked towards him. Towering over him, the man bent down.

The cub's hair bristled. His lips went into a snarl, showing his little fangs.*

The man laughed. 'Look!' he called to his friends. 'White fangs!' And he stretched out his hand. The cub lay still until the hand touched him. Then he lashed out and sank his teeth into the man's fingers. At once he received a sharp smack on his head.

At that, all the fight went out of him. He sat down and wailed his terror and his hurt. The men laughed. But then he heard his mother coming!

She-wolf bounded up, snarling and showing her razor-like fangs. The cub gave a joyful little cry and scuttled to meet her. The man-animals backed off hastily.

Then a cry went up from one of the men. 'Kiche!' The cub felt his mother quiver at the sound. 'Kiche!' said the man again, sharply.

At once, his mother – the she-wolf, the fearless one – crouched down on her belly. She wagged her tail, making peace signs.

The cub could not understand it. These strange creatures must be all-powerful for his mother to behave like this.

The men crowded round She-wolf. They stroked and patted her, and she didn't resist. The cub crouched by his mother, and did his best to copy her.

'It is Kiche,' said one of the men called Grey Beaver.* 'Her father was a wolf, but her mother was a dog.'

'It's a year since she ran away,' said another man called Three Eagles. 'She has lived with wolves. See, this cub is the result of it.'

'It is plain that his mother is Kiche,' said Grey Beaver, 'but his father was a wolf. Therefore, he has both wolf and dog in him too. Kiche was my brother's dog, and my brother is dead. So I claim this cub as mine.' He looked at the cub and smiled. 'His fangs are very white. I name him White Fang.'

Grey Beaver fetched a leather strap. He tied one end around Kiche's neck and the other around a tree. White Fang followed and

lay down beside his mother. Grey Beaver
reached down and rolled him on his back.
White Fang felt helpless, lying in such a silly
way and his whole wolf-nature rebelled
against it. He growled softly, but the
man-animal did not smack him. He just
laughed. Then all of a sudden, the hand
rubbed his tummy playfully and White Fang
felt a new feeling. It was pleasure!

And when the man rubbed behind his ears, the cub felt all his fear melt away.

After a while there were more noises. The rest of the tribe was returning. With them came some new animals.

White Fang had never seen dogs before, but knew that they were like his own kind. But not quite. The dogs smelled Kiche and her cub and attacked, biting and snapping at them. Kiche then fought for White Fang, and the cub could hear the shouts of the man-animals, and the yelps of the dogs as they were beaten away.

The noise died down. He saw again the power of men, and felt that they had been fair. The dogs had deserved to be beaten!

A small man-animal untied Kiche and led her away towards the village. White Fang followed, feeling worried and uncomfortable at this new adventure.

He was awe-struck at the village, and its towering tepees.*

He was just gathering up the courage to explore, when a puppy, larger and older than he was, came swaggering towards him. The puppy's name was Lip-lip and he was a bully.

Lip-lip curled his lips and snarled. So White Fang did the same. They circled each other, bristling and snapping. White Fang was starting to enjoy himself – it was a sort of game. Then suddenly, without warning, Lip-lip leaped at him, slashing his leg. Yelping with shame, the little cub ran back to his mother, who had been tied to another tree at the end of a long leash.

Later that day, White Fang was watching Grey Beaver doing something with sticks and branches. There was a strange mist rising from the pile of wood. Then suddenly a living thing appeared, brilliant orange, twisting and turning. The cub had never seen fire, but he was drawn towards it. He crawled towards the flame. He heard Grey Beaver make a chuckling noise, and knew the sound was friendly.

Then White Fang's nose touched the fire. The savage orange thing attacked his nose! He scrambled back, crying in pain. His mother heard his cries and strained, uselessly, to rescue him. But Grey Beaver laughed and laughed, and called the rest of the camp to watch. Soon they were all laughing at poor little White Fang, with his burned nose.

It was the worst pain he had ever known. But the more he cried, the more the man-animals laughed. And then he felt ashamed. He now knew what laughter meant – that they thought him foolish. He fled once again to his mother, the one creature in the world who was not laughing.

Night came. White Fang lay by his mother's side, longing for the quiet of the stream and their cosy cave. There were too many of these dogs and man-animals, all squabbling and snapping and making a noise.

He watched the man-animals. They were wonder-workers, magic makers and had power over all things, alive and not alive. They could make that vicious thing called fire!

CHAPTER 6

Outcast!

The more White Fang learned about man-animals, the more he respected them. When they walked, he got out of their way. When they called his name, he went to them. When they were angry, he hid. He belonged to them as the dogs belonged to them. They were gods and he was in their power.

But the bully Lip-lip made his life miserable. Older and stronger, the puppy had chosen White Fang as his victim. He was never happier than when he was tormenting the newcomer.

White Fang would have loved to join in with the other puppies, playing and running together. But as soon as White Fang appeared, Lip-lip would attack him and drive him away.

After some months, Grey Beaver decided that Kiche would not run away, and he set her free. White Fang was thrilled. As long as he stayed by her side, Lip-lip wouldn't dare come near.

One morning soon after this, White Fang saw the man-animal, Three Eagles, loading a canoe. All of a sudden, his mother was taken aboard too. White Fang rushed after her, but the canoe sped off.

Wild with panic, the cub jumped in the water and swam after it. Grey Beaver called him back, but he was so scared of losing his mother, he didn't take any notice.

Then Grey Beaver jumped into another canoe and set off after him. When he caught the cub he gave him a terrible beating. White Fang cried and cried with pain.

That night, he thought of his mother and howled so loudly that he woke Grey Beaver. The man-animal came over and beat him again! White Fang learned then that men could be very cruel and he wanted to run away. But the memory of his mother held him back. He would stay and wait for her, however long it took.

Now White Fang's mother could no longer protect him, Lip-lip bullied him all the time. Soon White Fang began to grow more savage and cunning.

If there was trouble in the camp, whether it was fighting among the dogs, squabbling among the man-animals, or a piece of stolen meat,

White Fang usually got the blame.

The other dogs knew that he was different. They sensed a wildness in him that they did not have themselves. It was a hard time for White Fang. The tooth of every dog was against him, and he was always ready for an attack.

But White Fang had the spirit of his mother and his father, the battle-scarred One-eye. However often he was beaten by Lip-lip, nothing could crush this.

CHAPTER 7

Friends and enemies

White Fang never forgot his mother, or stopped longing for the wilderness of his early cubhood, but by and by, he began to settle down. Grey Beaver never petted him again, but he sometimes threw him a hunk of meat, and shooed away the other dogs if they tried to steal it.

That winter, Grey Beaver set out on a long trip overland with his big sled,* while his young son Mit-sah had a smaller one pulled by a team of puppies.

There were seven puppies in Mit-sah's team, including White Fang. The leader was

White Fang's old enemy Lip-lip!

At first Lip-lip thought it an honour to be leader – but he soon found it was the worst place to be. All day long, the other dogs were snapping at his heels. Worse still, Mit-sah gave him extra meat in front of the other dogs and they hated him for it.

Lip-lip became an outcast,* just as he had once made White Fang.

One day, Mit-sah was collecting firewood in the forest when a gang of boys from another tribe* attacked him. A mad rush of anger rose in White Fang. Mit-sah, his master, was being hurt!

He leaped at the boys, snarling and snapping, and they fled in terror.

When Mit-sah told the story in camp, Grey Beaver gave White Fang a huge piece of meat.

The cub then lay down, full and happy, by the fire. He had just learned a valuable new lesson. Protect your master and you will be rewarded.

When spring came, Grey Beaver and his team went back home. White Fang was now a year old. Although a long way from being fully-grown, after Lip-lip, he was the biggest yearling in camp.

As the months went by, White Fang grew even stronger. From his mother, he had a dog's size and cleverness, and from his father, the cunning and strength of a wolf.

When White Fang was three years old there was a great famine in the camp. There was no food, not even for the man-animals, and the old and the weak were dying from hunger. Several dogs, including White Fang, ran off into the forest to find food for themselves.

Time passed, then one day, White Fang was out hunting when he sensed something behind him. He knew the scent, and it was not pleasant. He turned. A dog stood on the path in front of him. It was his old enemy, Lip-lip!

The two animals stared at each other. The hairs on White Fang's back bristled and the old anger flooded back. He snarled.

Lip-lip backed away, then White Fang sprang at him, knocking him to the ground. He showed no mercy to the old bully. He was even at last.

Not long after this, he returned to the village. The famine was over and he smelled food! He trotted boldly into Grey Beaver's tepee. Mit-sah welcomed him with happy cries and gave him a whole fish.

CHAPTER 8

The Fighting Wolf

When White Fang was five years old, Grey Beaver set off on the long journey to Fort Yukon* to sell furs. White Fang was now head of the dog team and was a fast and fearless leader. When they arrived, he saw more man-animals than he had seen in his life. Many of them had pale skin.

Every few days a steamship* would arrive
and the pale man-animals would come ashore
with their dogs. These were soft, silly creatures
that made a lot of noise. However, some made
the mistake of trying to attack White Fang.

He enjoyed this game.

As they rushed at him, he would spring to
one side. While they stood stupidly wondering
where he had gone, he would knock them
off their feet. He could have killed them with
one slash of his teeth. But White Fang was
cunning. He knew that man-animals were

angry when their dogs were killed. So he slunk away and let other dogs race in for the kill. They were the ones who were punished, not him.

Sometimes, the men who lived at the fort came down to see this wolfish dog, which was never wrong-footed. But the man who loved the dog fights more than any other was 'Beauty' Smith. He would run down at the first sound of the steamship's whistle. No one knew Beauty's real name, but he was far from beautiful, and a cowardly, cruel bully.

Beauty Smith was thrilled by White Fang's strength and cunning. And he also saw that he could make a lot of money from him.

Beauty knew that White Fang belonged to Grey Beaver. He took to visiting him, offering money. But Grey Beaver refused. White Fang was the strongest sled dog he had ever owned and the best leader. There was no dog like him anywhere in the country.

No. White Fang was not for sale!

But Beauty Smith was cunning. Every visit

he brought whiskey for Grey Beaver, and
one day he tricked him into selling his dog.
White Fang hated this new, pale man-animal.
Something told him that Beauty was bad
through and through. But he couldn't know
that the day Beauty took him away would be
the worst in his life.

Beauty Smith was cruel beyond anything
White Fang had ever known and the worst
kind of coward. He was too scared to fight a
man, but with a heavy club, he felt powerful
enough to beat a dog.

Beauty chained White Fang in a pen* so he could hardly move. He teased and taunted him until the dog went into a rage. Then he beat him without mercy.

White Fang learned to hate as he had never hated before.

Beauty was doing this for a reason. One day, some men came to the pen. Beauty took the chain from White Fang's neck. The dog was mad with spitting, snarling rage. A fighting dog* in peak condition.

The door of the pen opened. White Fang

stopped for a second, puzzled. Then another dog was shoved inside! It was huge. White Fang leaped at it with a flash of fangs that ripped at the dog's throat. The dog lunged at White Fang, but the wolf-dog was too clever. He leaped in again, slashing with his fangs. And the other dog lunged no more.

The men cheered and clapped. Big as he was, the other dog had had no chance. Beauty Smith grinned from ear to ear.

White Fang began to look forward to these fights. This was the only time he was ever free from his chain. One day, three dogs were put against him in a row. On another day, a full-grown wolf. Then two dogs were set on him at once. Sometimes White Fang would be injured, but Beauty did not care. He was becoming rich, betting on his dog.

Soon White Fang was famous. They called him 'The Fighting Wolf'.

When the first snows came, Beauty locked him in a cage and took him up river to Dawson* town.

There, men paid to stare at him and poke him with sticks. He raged and snarled at them. Hate had become his whole life, and why not? Life had become a living hell.

Dog fighting was against the law in that town, and so Beauty would take him into the woods at night. Men brought their most ferocious dogs to challenge 'The Fighting Wolf'. It was a savage land, and the fights were to the death.

But White Fang was never beaten.

Soon, dog owners did not want to risk their dogs against him. So Beauty set a full-grown lynx on him. White Fang fought like a demon – and won.

Then one day a gambler called Tim Keenan arrived in Dawson. He owned the first bulldog* that had ever been seen in that country.

It was clear that White Fang would have to fight this strange, powerful-looking dog, and for days people talked of nothing else.

CHAPTER 9

White Fang fights for his life

In the forest, Beauty Smith unchained his dog
and stood back. For once, White Fang didn't
make the first move. He was puzzled. This
dog wasn't like any dog he'd ever seen. It was
short and squat and hairless. It just stood still
and stared at White Fang.

The crowd yelled, 'Go get him, Cherokee! Eat him up!'

But Cherokee turned his head and blinked, wagging his tail. Tim Keenan started talking to his dog in a low voice. The bulldog began to growl. Then White Fang sprang. The crowd gasped. White Fang had moved more like a cat than a dog, slashing at the bulldog with his deadly fangs and leaping away.

The bulldog was bleeding, but he didn't even snarl! He just walked towards White Fang. Again White Fang sprang in, wounding the bulldog. But the bulldog came after him, slowly and steadily. He had something to do, and nothing could stop him.

White Fang was confused. This dog didn't

seem to notice his attacks.

Then White Fang tried to knock the bulldog over. This was usually how he won his fights. He struck. But the bulldog was much shorter than the other dogs White Fang had fought. He missed the dog and lost his footing.

At that instant, Cherokee's teeth gripped White Fang's throat and hung on. The crowd went wild. For the first time, it seemed that White Fang might be beaten!

White Fang jumped up. He tried to shake the bulldog off. He was frantic. A great weight was dragging him down, choking him. Round and round he went, like a mad thing. But Cherokee knew he was doing right by hanging on. He would never let go!

Each time White Fang hesitated, the bulldog sunk his teeth deeper. White Fang was getting tired. He couldn't get free and he couldn't understand why. Then he fell. The bulldog shifted his grip, getting in closer. Those who had bet on Cherokee began to cheer. It looked as if the fight was over.

At that moment, two men with a sled arrived and came over to see what was happening.

White Fang had almost stopped struggling. His eyes were glazing over. Beauty knew the fight was lost and he would have to pay out a lot of money. He sprang into the ring cursing and yelling. As White Fang lay helpless, he began kicking him. The crowd hissed at him. This was cruelty, and to his own dog!

One of the newcomers, a tall young man, pushed through the crowd.

Beauty was just about to give another kick when the newcomer's fist landed in his face.

He staggered and fell in the snow.

'Coward!' shouted the young man, Scott, in a rage, his grey eyes flashing.

He called to his friend, and both men bent over the dogs. The older man, Matt, took hold of White Fang. The younger man then tried to pull the bulldog's jaws apart.

The crowd began to jeer. No one came to help them.

'You'll have to use a stick,' said Matt.

Then Cherokee's owner, Tim Keenan, came forward. 'Don't you touch my dog, stranger!'

'So this is *your* dog,' replied Scott. 'Break his grip, or I will!'

Tim Keenan didn't move. So Scott thrust the stick into the bulldog's jaws. He worked away gently, loosening the jaws a bit at a time.

Suddenly, White Fang was free. Tim Keenan picked up the struggling Cherokee and strode away into the crowd.

White Fang tried to get up, but his legs were too weak. 'He's not good,' said Matt, 'but he's still alive.'

Scott glared at Beauty Smith. 'I'll give you a hundred and fifty dollars for him.'

'I ain't selling,' muttered Beauty.

'Oh, yes you are!' said Scott coldly. He opened his wallet and counted out the notes. 'You don't deserve to own this dog. Or any dog.'

Coward that he was, Beauty slunk off without a word. He knew he was beaten.

CHAPTER 10

There's no taming him!

Scott looked at White Fang snarling at the end of his chain. 'It's hopeless,' he said. 'He's a wolf and there's no taming him.'

'But look at those marks across his chest,' said Matt. 'I reckon he's already been tamed.'

'You're right,' said Scott. 'He must have been a sled dog before that brute Beauty Smith got hold of him.'

Matt undid the chain. White Fang got up warily, expecting to be beaten at any moment.

'Won't he try to escape?' said Scott.

'Might and might not,' said Matt. 'Set him free and we'll find out.'

'Poor devil,' said Scott. 'What he needs is some human kindness.'

He fetched a piece of meat from the cabin and threw it at the dog.

White Fang eyed it. He trusted nothing and no man.

One of the sled dogs was already moving towards the meat. 'Leave it, Major!' warned Matt.

But Major took no notice and sprang forward. In a flash, White Fang struck out. Matt leaped in, but too late, and Major lay bleeding in the snow. Matt went to slap White Fang. There was another sudden leap, a flash of fangs.

Matt looked at his bleeding leg. 'He got me all right,' he said.

'Only one thing to be done,' said Scott sadly. He reached for his gun. 'But we've got to do it.'

'Look here, Mr Scott,' said Matt. 'That poor creature's been through hell. You can't expect him to be an angel overnight. He needs time.'

'But he bit you!' said Scott. 'He's too dangerous. It'd be a mercy to kill him.'

Matt looked at White Fang. 'Give him a chance. If he don't come good, I'll kill him myself. How's that?'

'OK,' agreed Scott. 'But let me try this time.'

Scott went up to White Fang, who watched him warily. He'd attacked this man's dog and bitten his friend. Some terrible punishment must be coming.

Scott reached out his hand. White Fang snarled and struck with the speed of a coiled snake. Scott yelped.

'That's it!' cried Matt. He dashed into the cabin and returned with a rifle.

'What are you doing?' cried Scott.

'Keeping my promise,' said Matt.

'No!' said Scott. 'Look at him!'

White Fang was now watching Matt and snarling.

'He's clever,' said Scott. 'He knows what you're doing.'

Matt lifted the rifle and aimed. White Fang sprang sideways and tried to hide behind the cabin.

'Well, I'll be...' cried Matt, amazed. 'You're right. That dog is too clever to kill!'

CHAPTER 11

Love

White Fang was wary. He was still waiting for his punishment. He watched the men. At first they put some meat near him in the snow. He went up to it, expecting a trick. But nothing happened. He ate the meat. Then one of the men came near with more meat in his hand. White Fang stared at it. Was *this* the trick? Bit by bit, he went up to the man, keeping his eyes firmly fixed on him. Finally, he took the meat and growled, to show he wasn't to be tricked!

The man started talking to him in a soft voice. It gave White Fang a strange feeling, as if an empty space inside him was being filled. Then the hand came again. Immediately he was wary. Now it was coming. The punishment!

But the man went on talking in that soft tone. White Fang was torn, the voice made him feel calm, but the hand was a threat. He snarled and flattened his ears. Nearer and nearer, the hand came, and then it touched his fur. He shrank down. It followed him, stroking and patting him and rubbing his ears.

'Well, I never!' said Matt, scratching his head, puzzled.

White Fang snarled at the sound of Matt's voice, but he did not leap away from the hand that was stroking him.

This was the beginning of a new life for White Fang. For Scott it meant hours of hard work and patience. For White Fang it was the end of a life of hate.

But things do not happen in a day. Scott was determined to use kindness to awaken White Fang's need to love and be loved. Once, White Fang had known this with his mother, but a life of hardship and cruelty had made him unloving and unlovable.

Every day, Scott spent time, stroking and

patting him. White Fang still had his ferocious growl, but Scott noticed a new note – a purr of content.

Slowly, White Fang came to trust Scott. He took it upon himself to guard his master's things, and while he was there, no man would dare to steal from his cabin. And when he was ready to work again, White Fang took leadership of the sled pack.

Then something terrible happened. His master disappeared!

He had noticed him packing his bags. But he had not understood what it meant. That night, he stayed awake waiting in vain for his master to return. He wasn't to know that Scott had gone south to see his family.

Days came and went and still Scott didn't come back. White Fang became sick, so sick that Matt had to bring him inside the cabin. In the end, Matt wrote to Scott:

'That old wolf won't work. Won't eat. Ain't got no life left in him. Wants to know where you are. Reckon he'll pine away* and die.'

One night, Matt was reading when he was
startled by a low whine from White Fang. The
dog stood up, and stared at the door. A few
moments later there was a footstep. The door
opened and Scott stepped in.

'Where's the wolf?' he said. Then he saw
him, standing near the stove. He had not run
forward, but stood watching and waiting.

'Well, I never!' cried Matt. 'Look – he's
wagging his tail!'

Scott strode across the room, calling to
his dog.

White Fang came to him.

He was awkward and shy, but as he drew closer his eyes looked full of light.

Scott squatted on his heels. Face to face with his dog, he petted him, rubbing his ears and stroking his back. White Fang responded with a funny, purring growl. But that was not all. He suddenly thrust his head forward and nudged his way between his master's arm and body. Here, all but his ears hidden from view, he nestled and snuggled.

The two men looked at each other. Scott's eyes were shining.

'D'you see that?' said Scott. 'Lucky I could get back for a couple of months!'

With the return of his beloved master, White Fang got well quickly. He bounded out to meet the other sled dogs. Now he was king again!

CHAPTER 12

Going home

Something was in the air. White Fang knew it. All his senses told him that some big change was about to come.

'Listen to that, will you,' said Matt one night.

Scott listened. Through the open door came a low, anxious whine, like a sobbing under the breath. Then came a long sniff, as White Fang looked at his master, checking he was still there.

'I reckon that dog's on to you,' said Matt.

Scott looked at his friend sadly. 'I can't stay any longer. I've got a new job in California.'

How could I look after a wolf-dog there?' he said. 'He would hate living in a city, anyway.'

Matt looked at him. 'That dog loves you,' he said.

Scott glared across the table. 'Don't make me feel bad! I've got to do what I think is best!'

The truth was that Scott was torn. He was miserable at the idea of leaving White Fang, but he knew a dog like him needed the wide-open spaces of the frozen North. Five or six times he changed his mind. But in the end he decided firmly against taking him.

Then came the day when through the cabin door White Fang saw his master packing his bags. This was just like last time! Except that this time, he knew what it meant. His master was going away and leaving him behind!

Inside the cabin, the two men were getting ready for bed. 'He's gone off his food again,' said Matt.

'Don't say another word,' said Scott.

The next day, White Fang's fears grew and

grew. He wouldn't leave his master's side for a
second, and when Scott went inside, he stood
outside by the door, watching his every move.
Then Scott took his two large bags out of the
cabin, followed by a tin box. Now there was
no doubt. The terrible thing was happening.

White Fang watched as two men arrived.
They took the bags away down the hill
towards the steamship port.

Scott called White Fang. 'Poor fellow,' said
Scott, gently rubbing White Fang's ears. 'I'm

hitting the trail, old boy, where you can't follow. Now give me one of your growls, the last. A goodbye growl!'

But White Fang wouldn't growl. He gave his master a wistful, searching look and buried his head out of sight, between his master's arm and body.

A ship's horn sounded. 'There she blows!' said Matt. 'You've got to go now. You don't want to miss the boat!'

The two men closed up the cabin. Matt locked the door. From inside, came a low whining and sobbing.

Scott wiped his eyes. 'Take good care of him, Matt,' he said. 'Write and let me know how he gets on.'

'Sure,' replied Matt. 'But listen to that, will you?'

Both men stopped. White Fang was howling as dogs howl when their masters die. His cry burst upwards, dying down into quavering misery. A heart-breaking cry, it rose up again and again.

◆◆◆

The steamship was jammed with passengers.
Near the gangplank,* Scott was saying goodbye
to Matt. As Matt got ready to go ashore,
they had a final handshake. But Matt's hand
dropped.

He stared at something behind them. Scott
turned to see.

Sitting on the deck of the steamship,
watching wistfully was White Fang!

'Did you lock the door?' asked Scott.

'Sure did,' said Matt.

White Fang flattened himself to the ground,
his ears back. He felt desperate.

Matt tried to catch him to take him ashore,
but in a second he ran off into the crowd of
passengers. It was only when Scott called that
he came to them.

As Scott patted the dog, he noticed
something. He bent in closer and saw blood on
his muzzle* and a fresh cut between his eyes.

'We forgot the window!' he cried.

'He's all cut up. Must have butted his way clean through the glass. I don't believe it!'

The steamship hooted its final whistle.

'I'd better have him now,' said Matt.

'Goodbye, Matt,' said Scott, taking no notice. 'I'll write to you about the dog.'

'You don't mean…'

'I do!' said Scott firmly. 'I'm taking him with me.'

The gangplank was hauled in and the steamship swung out from the bank. Scott waved a last goodbye to Matt on the shore. Then he bent down to White Fang. 'Growl for me *now*, won't you, you stupid, brave fellow!' he said.

White Fang knew he had won. He growled and purred and nuzzled his beloved master for all he was worth.

Jack London

(born 1876, died 1916)

Jack London grew up just outside San Francisco in America, in a poor family. He took his surname from his stepfather. Jack went to primary school, but mostly taught himself at the local library when he was not helping on the family farm.

At the age of 13 he worked 12–18 hours a day in a canning factory. It was hard work, so he borrowed some money, bought a boat, and fished for oysters. Later he worked as a sailor, travelling as far as Japan. When he came back to America there were few jobs. He wandered around with no money and no job. He was put in jail for a month for having no place to live.

After all this, at 19, he went home and finally went to secondary school. He started to write short stories about the things he knew.

At the age of 21, Jack heard that gold had been discovered in the far north of America, on the border with Canada. He went looking for gold, but found only a cold, harsh frozen landscape. When he got home he decided the only way to stop being poor was to 'sell his brains', so he began to sell his short stories. In a short space of time he became one of the richest writers in America.

Best known works
The Call of the Wild
The Sea-Wolf

Caroline Castle

Caroline Castle worked in publishing for many years before becoming a full time author in 2006. Her fiction titles include the bestselling *Letters of a Lovestruck Teenager* (written under the pen name Claire Robertson), *Rosie Pugh and the Great Clothes War,* and most recently *Tales of Beauty and Cruelty* co-written with Kate Petty. Caroline lives in Camden, north London. She says, *'White Fang,* the magnificent story of a little wolf cub's struggle for survival as he grows up in the Canadian wilderness, was both a challenge and a joy to retell. Full of life and death suspense, it is a page-turning adventure that no one should miss.'

Alison Sage

Alison Sage has spent her working life in children's books, mostly as an editor but also as an author of several children's books including the *Hutchinson Treasury of Children's Literature.* She is married with three children.

She says, 'When I was about nine, my best friend had a dog called Rebel. He was odd-looking and disobedient but my friend fell in love with him, and I loyally fell in love with him too. Together we tried to train Rebel and although I can't say that he became a miracle of good behaviour, he was adored by everyone.'

'My friend chose Rebel because he'd read a book called *White Fang*, about a wild dog whose life turned around because he had an owner who loved him. I read *White Fang* too, and although I was also horrified at the cruelty and hardship that he suffered, I never forgot it.'

Notes about this book

This book is unusual because some of it is written from the point of view of the wolf-dog, White Fang. This lets us think about how dogs might feel, and how they might look at the world and at people.

The story is set at the end of the 19th century, about the time when Jack London went north in search of gold. He was one of over 40,000 people who joined a 'gold rush' to the frozen north looking for a fortune.

The setting of the book, on the border of Canada and Alaska (USA), is almost permanently covered in snow. Before the invention of cars and snowmobiles, the way to get about was by dog power. You would pack a whole year's worth of supplies on to a sled and journey across the frozen land pulled by a team of dogs. The few towns in the area, like Fort Yukon and Dawson, were the only places where you could trade, or get a bath!

White Fang was made into a film in 1991.

Page 9
* **she-wolf** A female wolf.

Page 13
* **instinct** Behaviour that comes naturally.

Page 16
* **lynx** A medium-sized type of wild cat.
* **lair** The place where a wild animal lives.

Page 21
* **famine** A severe shortage of food.

Page 23
*__fought like demons__ To fight madly.

Page 26
*__fangs__ Sharp teeth.

Page 28
*__Grey Beaver__ This is the kind of name Native Americans had. They often used animal names.

Page 31
*__tepees__ Native American tents, usually in the shape of a cone, made with animal skins.

Page 38
*__sled__ Sometimes called a sledge, this is a vehicle for travelling over snow that has strips of metal or wood called runners, for sliding along.

Page 39
*__outcast__ Someone who has been rejected by a family or group.
*__tribe__ A group of families living together. They were not always friendly with other tribes.

Page 42
*__Fort Yukon__ A town (now a city) in Alaska, USA.

Page 43
*__steamship__ A ship driven by steam. The ship in this story would journey up the Yukon River from the Alaskan coast. It would bring food and supplies up to Fort Yukon and other towns, and take furs and other goods downriver to be sold elsewhere.

Page 46
*__pen__ An enclosure for animals.
*__fighting dog__ Some people train dogs to fight other dogs and bet money on which dog will win. Dog fighting is illegal today in most countries.

Page 47
*__Dawson__ A town (now a city) in Canada.

Page 49
*__bulldog__ A breed of medium-sized dog with a short thick neck and short stocky legs.

Page 64
*__pine away__ To be so upset, often when someone leaves or dies, that a person or animal becomes weaker and weaker.

Page 68
*__California__ A southern state (part) of the USA, far away from snowy Alaska in the far North.

Page 72
*__gangplank__ A moveable plank used by passengers for walking on or off a ship.
*__muzzle__ An animal's nose and mouth. (It is also the word for a device that fits over an animal's mouth to stop it from biting.)